My name is Jessica Frew, and I'm The author of *The Nonverbal Princess*. I'm 21 years old. Due to my CP, I have Cerebral Palsy and communicate with a Tobii eye gaze computer. I'm a model/actress in the entertainment/fashion industry and a freshman at William Paterson University for Criminal Justice. *The Nonverbal Princess* is more than just some children's fairy tale because people have treated me differently since I was young and thought I wouldn't know anything because I was nonverbal. Hence, people used to say very mean stuff right before me without realizing I could understand everything they were saying, making me feel worthless. I didn't even have the confidence to communicate with my computer in public or even with my family; I just used it for school work Until I found the confidence in myself. I want to teach children around the world that people with disabilities or differences who look or act differently are humans with emotions too.

Copyright © Jessica Frew 2024

All rights reserved. No part of this publication may be reproduced, distributed, or transmitted in any form or by any means, including photocopying, recording, or other electronic or mechanical methods, without the prior written permission of the publisher, except in the case of brief quotations embodied in critical reviews and certain other non-commercial uses permitted by copyright law. For permission requests, write to the publisher.

Any person who commits any unauthorized act in relation to this publication may be liable to criminal prosecution and civil claims for damages.

Ordering Information

Quantity sales: Special discounts are available on quantity purchases by corporations, associations, and others. For details, contact the publisher at the address below.

Publisher's Cataloging-in-Publication data

Frew, Jessica

The Nonverbal Princess

ISBN 9781647503376 (Paperback)
ISBN 9781647503543 (Hardback)
ISBN 9781647503567 (ePub e-book)

Library of Congress Control Number: 2023924217

www.austinmacauley.com/us

First Published 2024
Austin Macauley Publishers LLC
40 Wall Street, 33rd Floor, Suite 3302
New York, NY 10005
USA

mail-usa@austinmacauley.com
+1 (646) 5125767

I created *The Nonverbal Princess* for individuals with disabilities who fear being belittled, judged, and looked down upon by society whenever they leave their houses. To show them it doesn't matter what other individuals think about us; what matters is what you feel about yourself and have the confidence to speak up for yourself.

I want to give a special thanks to Aware Ties for backing and believing in *The Nonverbal Princes*, Joe Leone for making the initial edits, and Gustavo Vera for the amazing illustration ideas. I also want to give thanks to Austin Macaulay Publishers for publishing and bringing *The Nonverbal Princess* to life.

Once upon a time, in the fair kingdom of Elesia, the queen and king were about to have their first child. When the queen was ready to deliver the baby, the doctor made a bad mistake, which caused the queen and her baby to die. But then, a miracle happened. Three angels brought the little princess back to life because they knew that she was going to be very special. However, the little princess now had a disability called cerebral palsy. Although the king was hurting over the death of the queen, when he looked into the princess's eyes, his pain melted away. He said, "I know you have a long journey ahead of you, but I believe you will fight through the challenges, and you will be queen one day."

As the years went by, the princess grew up to be a very bright young lady. She spoke to the king and the members of the court using a special computer that she controlled with her eyes. She got around using a motorized wheelchair. Yet, many of the villagers thought that the princess was not smart. They thought that she was helpless, just staring off into space, with no thoughts in her head at all. Because of this, they treated her very badly. They spoke to her like she was just a little baby, and some of them even said cruel things about the princess right in front of her as if she couldn't even hear them. This made the princess very sad, and caused her to feel quite bad about herself, and her disability.

One day, the princess came back to the castle after watching wild horses play in a field. She rode in her wheelchair towards her bedroom, and when she passed by her father's quarters, she heard another person's voice. The voice belonged to a powerful man, the ping of Phonecia. The Phonecian king angrily said to her father, "Your daughter can never be queen. She can't even speak normally. When she was born with such a horrible disability, you should have had the doctor drown her right then and there." When she heard that, the princess drove her wheelchair into her room and shut the door behind her. There, she cried and cried and cried.

In her mind, the princess thought, "Everyone thinks I am helpless, and I have no real voice in the kingdom. Why should I even try?" The princess's sadness turned to anger. She used all her strength to hit her computer screen off of its stand. It crashed down to the floor, and broke into a million tiny pieces. The princess just sat there, sulking.

Later that night, some of the castle's servants came into the princess's room. They told her that the king had fallen ill, and that she needed to go and see him, right away. The alarmed princess looked down at the busted computer screen on the floor. The servants understood that the princess could no longer operate her wheelchair, so they picked her up and hurriedly carried her into the king's room.

At the king's bedside, the princess was now seated. The servants explained to the king what happened to the princess's computer and chair. The sickly king then got a sad, heavy look on his face. He asked the princess, "Did you overhear my conversation before with the king of Phonecia?" The princess simply shook her head up and down, signaling 'Yes.' The king then looked her right in the eyes and said, "People will say hurtful things, especially those who have power in the kingdom, because they want you to feel down about yourself. They want you to give up because that makes it easier for them to rule. Do you

know how often people said I did a horrible job while I was king?" The princess shook her head "No." The king gave her a small grin and said, "Let's just say: a lot. But every time they say something bad about me, it goes in one ear, and out the other. That's because it doesn't matter what people think about you—all that matters is what you think about yourself." The princess smiled back. But right then, the king passed away. The princess was broken-hearted, and felt all alone.

For the next few weeks, the princess stayed in her room. There she remained, crying and feeling awful. The servants tried everything they could to get her to come out, but she just refused. Since the king's death, his sister, Viviana, had returned to Elesia. She was a mean-spirited woman, who didn't care for the princess at all. Viviana only wanted to be queen so she could take the riches of the kingdom all for herself. Sadly, the people of Elesia needed someone to rule the kingdom, and so they were going to crown Viviana as their queen. This was to happen in a few days, and the princess's time to claim her rightful throne was quickly running out.

The night before Viviana's coronation was to take place, the princess was in her room, crying herself to sleep. Just then, three angels appeared to her. The princess was very surprised. In her mind, she asked, "Who are you?"

All three of the angels were able to read her mind. One of them replied, "You probably don't remember us, for you were only a tiny baby when we met you." The princess gazed at them, very confused.

Another angel then said "We saved you. We brought you back to life." The princess stared at them, in shock.

The third angel then asked her, "Do you know why we saved you then, and have come to see you again tonight?" The princess simply shook her head "No."

The first angel smiled warmly, and explained, "Your life is destined for a very special purpose. You must become the new queen. You have the power to be a voice for the thousands of villagers in the land with disabilities. You can reunite the entire kingdom of Elesia, and everyone shall then be treated as equals." Hearing this, the princess peered at them, now with hope in her eyes.

The second angel looked down at her and said, "Your parents sent us here tonight, to give you this message. Your father wanted us to remind you that people will try to knock you down, but you must get back up—and face every new challenge even stronger. You just have to believe in yourself, and he will be with you each step of the way."

The princess frowned, and thought, "But how can I do any of that? My computer is broken, and the crowning is tomorrow. It is too late; my computer can never be fixed in that time!"

The angels smiled at one another. They raised their arms, and the broken pieces of the computer screen rose off the floor and swirled in the air. The princess watched this, completely amazed. Suddenly, the floating pieces all came together at once, and the computer screen was fixed as if it were new.

The first angel then spoke once more, "We have done this for you—but the rest, princess...that is up to you." The angels then all bowed their heads, and floated up to the ceiling. In a burst of bright white light, they then disappeared. The princess continued to stare in that direction, as she thought deeply about everything they had said.

The next morning, the princess emerged from her room. All of the servants were pleasantly shocked. The princess rode in her chair down the hallway. She passed by Viviana, who could barely believe her own eyes. The princess smiled, and made her way into the grandest room of the castle, where she was finally crowned the queen of Elesia. She then came to the balcony, and used her computer to speak out to the many villagers below. She told them all that Elesia has finally been reunited, and that every single person living there would be equal and free.

The crowd below cheered. The members of the royal court cheered. Even the princess's mean old aunt, Viviana, was moved by the princess's speech, and so she cheered for the princess as well.

The princess looked down at all the members of her kingdom, and smiled gratefully at them, ready for any new challenges that may come her way.

And they all lived happily ever after...

The End

Printed in the USA
CPSIA information can be obtained
at www.ICGtesting.com
LVHW061124200224
772325LV00003B/81